DISNEY's
Mickey Mysteries

MYSTERY OF THE GARBAGE GANG

DISNEY
PRESS

New York

Printed in the United States of America

First Edition
1 3 5 7 9 10 8 6 4 2

Library of Congress Catalog Card Number: 00-109809
ISBN 0-7868-4451-5

For more Disney Press fun, visit www.disneybooks.com

Chapter 1

MICKEY THE JOURNALIST

"Minnie," Mickey Mouse asked as he gazed at his partner's feet, "is it trendy to wear a pink shoe on one foot and an orange one on the other?"

Minnie looked at her shoes and sighed. "I'm afraid not," she admitted. "This is just like what I was telling you yesterday. I'm getting absentminded—I've been working too hard."

It had been a rough morning for Minnie already. First, she watered the plants at the Mickey and Minnie Detective Agency with window cleaner. Then, she forgot to save her

5

computer files and accidentally deleted two days' worth of work. "I can't keep up this pace much longer," she continued. "Ever since Inspector Sharp retired, it seems like all the lowlifes in the world have moved to town."

"What are you complaining about?" Mickey replied. "Business is booming! Besides, we *always* have a lot of work. After all, we're the best detectives in the city . . . maybe in the whole country."

"Yes, but—" A shrill ring cut Minnie off. "There's the phone again," she said with a groan. "It's been ringing off the hook. Let's stop answering it."

Mickey just laughed and picked up the phone.

"Hello?" he said. "Oh, good morning, Mr. Noble!" Mickey smiled, but his expression soon grew concerned. "What? What happened? You sound terrified. . . . Oh, I see, you've been receiving threats? Do you prefer to talk about it in person? . . . We can meet you at the newspaper offices in an hour. . . . Okay, see you soon!"

Mickey put the phone back in its cradle and began pacing the room, deep in thought.

"Who is Mr. Noble?" Minnie asked.

"He's the editor in chief of the newspaper, *The Herald*. He has a case for us."

"Great, that's all we need." Minnie rolled her eyes. "We already have more cases than we can handle. . . ."

"I know, I know. But how can we turn this one down?" Mickey shrugged. "Mr. Noble has always been a fearless crime fighter. He exposes injustices and catches criminals all over the city. . . ."

Minnie sighed. "You're right," she admitted. "Okay, here's an idea. You'll go to the appointment with Mr. Noble. In the meantime, I'll try to finish up our most urgent cases. I'll meet you as soon as I'm done . . . and I've changed my shoes."

"Sounds great," Mickey replied as he headed for the door. "If things are as bad as Mr. Noble made them sound, I'll really need your help."

When Mickey arrived at *The Herald*, he was

shown immediately to Mr. Noble's office. Mickey could read the fear and exhaustion in the editor's face.

"My dear Mickey," Mr. Noble explained, "*The Herald* is a paper that isn't afraid to expose injustice: we write the truth and nothing but the truth. Last year we exposed a restaurant for serving food that had gone bad. The owner had to pay a fine and clean up his act. A few months ago, we published a story on a dealer who sold cars that polluted the air. As a result, the dealership was closed. We've fought countless battles like these. And we always win!"

"And naturally," Detective Mickey said, "these kinds of stories don't exactly make you a lot a friends, right?"

"Right. A few of the people we've exposed truly hate us, and they often seek revenge," Mr. Noble said seriously. "We receive a lot of anonymous letters and telephone calls."

"Unfortunately that's one of the hazards of the job." Mickey shook his head.

"That's true," Mr. Noble admitted. "But no one has ever gone this far before."

Mickey frowned. "What do you mean, 'this far'?" he asked.

With a trembling hand, Mr. Noble pointed to a broken window.

"Someone tossed a rock through the window. There was a note attached." The editor opened a desk drawer and pulled out a piece of paper. "Whoever did this wants me to understand that this time the threats are serious. Here, read this."

He passed the note to the detective.

This is a warning.
If you publish one more word
against us, you can say good-bye
to your beloved newspaper.

Mickey couldn't hide his concern.

"Until today, none of the threats have ever been carried out," Mr. Noble explained, obviously disturbed. "But if they're bold enough to do this in broad daylight, who knows what they'll try next. . . ."

"We have to find whoever wrote this letter as soon as possible," Detective Mickey concluded. "We won't give him the chance to carry out any threats. Be brave, Mr. Noble. Starting now, the Mickey and Minnie Detective Agency is on the case."

Mr. Noble smiled. "You seem very sure of yourself," he said. "I like that. You have my permission to do whatever you think is necessary to take care of this situation. How do you plan to proceed?" he asked, leaning forward in his chair.

"Well, to start, my partner and I will pass ourselves off as your newest reporters. It will be much easier to observe any suspicious activity if we are working as journalists at *The Herald*."

"Great!" the editor exclaimed. "In fact, some of my reporters have left because they're worried about the threats. I can hire you to take their places and no one will suspect a thing."

Mickey knew that he could count on Minnie, but he thought this case might be too big for the two of them to handle on their own. He decided they would need help. Luckily, their good friends Horace Horsecollar and Goofy were available, and very eager to work for the newspaper. Goofy would work as a photojournalist, and Horace as a typist. Mickey also recruited Donald Duck to sell papers and write opinion pieces.

Overnight, it seemed that *The Herald's* new staff had made the paper better than ever. Detective Mickey was full of ideas for new columns. Clarabelle volunteered to cover the movie and theater sections, and Grandma Duck was going to share her best recipes. Mr. Noble was very pleased with all of the changes. He was certain that the newspaper's circulation would double in no time.

To be perfectly honest, there *was* the occasional disaster. Horace was a very *fast* typist, but not a very *accurate* typist. For example, Clarabelle's column, "Season's Best Films" became "Season's West Flims," while Grandma Duck's "Deviled Eggs" became "Reviled Legs." And Goofy's photos were almost always out of focus.

But these little details didn't seem so important. Donald had arranged for radio ads to publicize the latest edition of *The Herald*, and sales of the paper were on the rise. In fact, some readers bought *The Herald* just for the fun of finding typographical errors and figuring out what was pictured in Goofy's snapshots. It seemed everybody was reading the paper and congratulating Mr. Noble on his latest success.

Chapter 2

THE HAZARDS OF THE JOB

But Mickey was a private investigator, not a journalist! Even though he enjoyed writing for the paper, he was also working night and day to expose the criminals who had threatened the editor in chief.

Detective Mickey booted up his computer and began typing. Suddenly he heard a sound behind him. He turned and saw a tough-looking man in a leather jacket. He was glaring at Mickey as he chomped on a toothpick.

"Can I help you?" Mickey asked.

The man said nothing.

Mickey cleared his throat. "Can I help you?" he repeated. His voice was less friendly this time.

"Actually it's the other way around," the stranger replied. "You should be asking if *I* can help *you*."

"What do you mean?" Mickey asked.

"I came by here to offer the services of my company."

"I'm sorry, but if you're trying to sell

something, I'm not interested," Mickey replied, turning back to his computer.

"Just a minute," the man insisted. Mickey turned back to face him. "We offer a range of specialized services. We're a security agency. Lookout Security Services."

Detective Mickey folded his arms across his chest. "What type of protection do you offer?"

"Well, we live in dangerous times. . . ." the man said with a crooked smile. "And people like you, people in high-risk professions, have to be concerned with personal safety."

"What exactly do you mean by that?" Mickey demanded.

"Well, as I'm sure you're aware, there are people in this city who will do anything to protect their interests . . . they'll even go so far as to try to prevent journalists from exposing their shady business tactics."

"Well, they won't try anything with me," Mickey said firmly. "I'm more than capable of defending myself."

"Really?" the man replied. He looked Mickey up and down doubtfully. "Look, I don't know how long you've worked for the paper," he went on, "but without our protection, you won't go far in this career. You're in a very dangerous situation here."

"Well, maybe I like danger," Mickey said coolly. "And now, please leave me alone so I can get back to work!"

But the man wouldn't give up. "You're making a mistake," he said. "My team of bodyguards will protect you for just a thousand miserable bucks. . . ."

"Out!" Mickey shouted. "Or *you'll* be the one who needs protection!"

As soon as the stranger left his office, Mickey hurried to Mr. Noble's office to tell him about the unpleasant visit. Once Mickey had described the man from Lookout Security Services, he asked, "Do you know these people?"

Mr. Noble nodded. "Unfortunately, I do. I wrote an article on Lookout Security Services not long ago. I guess they didn't appreciate the negative publicity that the article generated. These thugs have struck gold. They sell their 'protective services' all over town, and they don't hesitate to use force against those who refuse to buy. I thought the police would take action, but Inspector Craven said that there wasn't enough evidence to bring them to trial."

"I've heard enough. We don't have any time to lose!" the detective cried.

Mickey rushed to the newsroom and asked Goofy to follow the rogue security officer. "He only left a moment ago," Mickey explained. "He couldn't have gone too far!"

"Aw, garsh," Goofy said, "I'm in the middle of developing these photos." Goofy was really enjoying his undercover assignment.

"That can wait," Mickey replied.

"But how will I recognize him?" Goofy asked.

"He's a big man, wearing jeans and leather boots."

Goofy thought a moment. "Are his jeans leather, too?"

"No, his jeans are . . . well, jeans! Only the boots are leather. And he has on a motorcycle

19

jacket with an owl design on the back. But you'd better hurry," Mickey urged, "or he'll get away!"

Goofy put aside his developing reluctantly. But once he was out of the building, it wasn't long before he was hot on the trail of the man with the motorcycle jacket.

"It's a good thing I brought my camera with me...." Goofy said to himself. "That way I can snap a photo of the man to give to the police."

The traffic light turned red just as the man in the leather jacket finished crossing the street. Goofy stopped short, his heart pounding, as the cars started to pull across the intersection—he was blocked!

When the light turned green, Goofy crossed the street and looked up and down the block. But the man wasn't there.

"Now what should I do? Mickey will be angry if I lose him," Goofy muttered. "I've got to find him again!"

Goofy walked halfway down the block and peered into a deserted alley.

Suddenly someone grabbed him from

behind and threw a sack over his head. Goofy felt himself being dragged across the alley, and heard the clang as someone shoved him into a garbage can. The metal lid landed heavily on Goofy's head as he heard a voice exclaim: "Tell the jerk who told you to follow me that he'd better get in touch with my boss. Otherwise you'll be hearing from me . . . and my associates!" Then Goofy heard two men laughing—someone was working with the man in the motorcycle jacket.

"Boss? What boss?" Goofy asked. But nobody answered him.

After a few minutes, Goofy managed to get the sack off his head. He looked around, but the street was deserted. The men were nowhere in sight.

Chapter 3

TROUBLE IN THE NEWSROOM

The following day, Mickey was still fuming over what had happened to Goofy. He decided to publish an editorial on a certain security agency's shady business practices.

It seems likely, Mickey wrote, *that the company is run by criminals. They make a killing offering people expensive protection . . . from themselves. When this paper tried to contact the owner of the business for comment, we discovered that nobody would admit to owning Lookout Security Services.*

The issue sold like crazy, which made

23

Mickey feel rather proud. After all, journalism is very much like detective work, and Mickey was glad that he was good at both.

Many readers were calling the paper to congratulate Mickey on his editorial, and he was so busy answering their calls that he barely had any time to work.

Luckily Minnie was there to keep things under control. While her partner talked on the phone and answered letters from readers, Minnie was typing up articles and keeping up on their casework.

"What's going on?" she asked suddenly, frowning at her monitor. "The screen just went blank! It must have come unplugged...."

Just as Minnie leaned down to check the cord, a huge rock burst through the window and shattered the computer screen into a million pieces. If she hadn't bent down at just that moment, the rock would have hit her in the head.

Mickey ran over. "Are you hurt?" he asked.

"No, I'm fine," Minnie said, staring at the rock. "Look at this." She leaned over to pick up the stone. "There's a message!"

The detective removed the heavy tape that held the message to the rock and unrolled the sheet of paper.

> *If you publish one more article*
> *about us, we'll put your*
> *newspaper through the shredder.*

"Who do these guys think they are?" Mickey growled.

"Well, at least this is proof against them," Minnie pointed out. "If Lookout Security Services were innocent, the president of the company would have come here in person to demand a retraction of the article, rather than sending an anonymous message."

"You're right," Mickey declared. "And if they think we can be so easily frightened by a rock and a note, they've got another thing coming!"

But perhaps Detective Mickey was a little too optimistic. The next day, when he and Minnie got into the newsroom, they found that the back door had been forced open.

Someone was guilty of breaking and entering—and Mickey was sure it was Lookout Security Services. But what had they been looking for? The notes for Mickey's next piece about their shady business? Fortunately, Mickey had taken the most important documents home and hidden them in a safe place.

Minnie sat down at her new computer. But when she tried to boot up, the screen flickered, then—*zap!*—the screen went blank.

Minnie was still puzzling over what could have gone wrong with her computer when Mickey tried to boot up. But—*zap!*—his machine stopped working too. Minnie hustled over to another computer. As she and Mickey tried every computer in the newsroom, they heard the now familiar *zap!* over and over.

"All the computers are fried," Minnie said with a sigh. "It'll be days before they can all be fixed. There's no way we'll get the next issue out on time. It's the work of that so-called security firm. I'd like to give them a piece of my mind...."

Mickey forced a smile.

"Now, Minnie, it won't do us any good to get angry. I know what we need to do. First of all, I'll call the computer repair service and have them send over their best technicians to work on getting the computers back in service. Then I'll type my article on my computer at the detective agency. I'll save it on a floppy disk and take it to the printer."

Minnie hugged him. "That's a great plan!" she cried. "Let's do it!"

"Aw, gee," Mickey said, and blushed. He went to the Mickey and Minnie Detective Agency and began to work on an editorial: *Who is the president of Lookout Security Services? It's only a matter of time before we discover his identity. We intend to gather evidence until we can prove that this company is the most dangerous enemy this city has ever had. And then the president of Lookout Security Services will go to trial for his crimes.*

By the time Mickey finished writing his editorial, it was late and Mickey had to get back to the newspaper offices so that the paper could go to press. Still, Mickey could have added a lot more to his article. . . .

Donald Duck made sure the papers were distributed to newsstands all over the city by delivering them himself. By the time Donald had finished, his feet were painfully swollen, but he was satisfied that he had done his part.

An hour later, in the newsroom, as Mickey was responding to the hundredth congratulatory phone call, he heard the door behind him creak open. Finally, he thought, the computer technicians are here. Mickey just hoped that they wouldn't tell him that all the computers had to be replaced.

Mickey turned. The man who had just entered his office, however, didn't look like a computer whiz. It was . . .

"Peg Leg Pete!" the detective exclaimed. "I thought you were in prison for trying to steal 'Mineshaft' Bill Pelton's gold."

The scoundrel laughed. "You thought wrong. I let my partner, Sylvester Slick, do the time in jail for me. It seemed that the police found plenty of evidence against him, and none against me. And here I am, my dear Mickey: Peg Leg Pete, the Generic Director—oops—I meant General Director of Lookout Security Services. I heard that you turned down our generous offer for discounted security. Not very nice of you . . . no . . . not nice at all. But I'm here to say that we can put that all behind us. Just give me the word and the capable staff of Lookout Security Services will become your own personal squadron of guardian angels."

"Not a chance," Mickey retorted. "I assure you, I can take care of myself. I don't need protection from you or your band of thugs."

But still Mickey's firm reply was not enough to discourage Peg Leg Pete.

"Just let me tell you one thing," Peg Leg Pete growled. "I've never let anyone interfere with my business affairs, and I don't intend to change my policy for a little pipsqueak like you!"

But Mickey was not so easily intimidated. He looked at Peg Leg Pete coolly. "Far be it from me to tell you how to run your business," he said. "If you have nothing to fear, why don't you follow me to the police inspector's office right now and make a statement."

Peg Leg Pete snorted. "Why would I do that?"

"You know exactly why," Mickey responded firmly. "Because your business is crooked. Come with me or I'll call the police!"

Peg Leg Pete just rolled his eyes and followed Mickey out the door. "Fine," Pete told the detective, "I'm not afraid of the police!"

Mickey frowned. Why had Peg Leg Pete agreed to come along so easily? It seemed out of character. He just hoped Peg Leg Pete didn't have an ace up his sleeve....

Chapter 4

AN UNSUSPICIOUS SUSPECT

It took a long time for the police officer to understand who Peg Leg Pete was and what Mickey was accusing him of.

"We'll begin our investigation immediately," the officer announced finally. "But of course you understand that we can't just arrest him now, without gathering evidence to establish that your accusations are true."

Peg Leg Pete snickered.

"All you have to do is come to the news-room of *The Herald*!" the detective replied, exasperated. "I'll show you the shattered computer monitor and the threatening messages. . . . And then there are all the malfunctioning computers. Just look around, and you'll see exactly what kind of kind of criminals we're dealing with here."

"Fine." The police officer pulled out some paperwork and began filling it out. "We'll need some time. . . ."

"Time?" Mickey pounded his fist against the police officer's desk. "In the time it takes

you to investigate who knows what he'll do! He has to be stopped—now!"

"Unfortunately, sir, you can only prove that your computers and window are broken, not that Peg Leg Pete is responsible," the officer explained. "We don't have a shred of evidence against him. But we can keep him under surveillance for twenty-four hours, which should be enough time for us to complete a preliminary investigation."

Mickey accepted the news calmly. He knew that once the police began their investigation, they would find more than enough reasons to keep Peg Leg Pete in prison for life.

"Just be careful not to lose sight of this man, even for a moment," Mickey warned the officer before he left. "He should be considered very dangerous."

The officer on duty didn't have time to respond before the phone rang. As Detective Mickey closed the door behind him, he heard the police officer say, "Yes, Inspector, of course. Certainly, Inspector Craven, I'll take care of it immediately."

Mickey breathed a sigh of relief. Now he

could move freely without running the risk of encountering one of Peg Leg Pete's goons. He decided he would run some errands that he had been putting off since he and Minnie took the case.

But when Mickey returned to his office a few hours later, who did he find sprawled out carelessly in the armchair by his desk?

Peg Leg Pete!

"What are you doing here?" the detective demanded. "I thought for sure you'd be in prison by now!"

"Oh, really?" Peg Leg Pete sounded bored. "Actually, they let me go after only a few minutes. . . . You didn't really think they'd keep me in there, did you?"

"Get out of here right now!" Mickey fumed, fed up with Peg Leg Pete's games.

"Not before telling you why I came," Peg Leg Pete replied. "Here's my message: calm down, forget about me, and, above all, never write another word about me or my business affairs in that paper of yours. Follow my advice, or, I assure you, you'll pay for it."

"I'll write whatever I want," Mickey said defiantly. "And believe me, I'll follow this story until the end!"

"As you like, Mickey! But believe me, you'll regret it."

Peg Leg Pete finally left, laughing all the way down the hall.

Mickey frowned. How did that good-for-nothing get out of prison? he wondered. There was no way he could've planned an escape in such a short time! Obviously the police had let him go. But why so soon?

All of a sudden the investigator remembered that just as he was leaving the police station, the officer on duty had received a phone call. But what had the inspector asked the officer to do? Inspector Sharp had been one of the best investigators Mickey had ever known. But he had retired recently, and Mickey didn't know Inspector Craven, Sharp's replacement. Was it possible that Inspector Craven was in cahoots with Peg Leg Pete? It seemed unlikely. Then again, why else would Peg Leg Pete have been released so soon?

Mickey decided that the best way to test his theory was to follow Peg Leg Pete. Besides, the computers wouldn't be back up until later that evening, so he couldn't get anything done at the paper.

Mickey was an ace at shadowing suspects. Peg Leg Pete never noticed that he was being followed, not even when he sat down at a café to have a root beer.

Just then, Mickey saw Inspector Craven approach Peg Leg Pete. The detective, who was well hidden behind a hedge, crept closer so he could hear what they were saying.

"At eight at the Oscar Cinemas," Inspector Craven said. "My man will be wearing a polka-dotted cap. You will hand him the package. And no tricks. I expect to be paid for my services."

Peg Leg Pete grinned. "Of course, Inspector. You can count on me."

Mickey was sure that the package they were discussing would contain a nice, fat payoff. It was obvious—Peg Leg Pete was paying Inspector Craven for keeping him out of prison. They were conspirators.

Detective Mickey made a decision. He would send Goofy to spy on the meeting between the inspector's colleague and Peg Leg Pete.

Chapter 5

SCOOP GETS THE SCOOP

"How was your evening at the movies, Goofy?" Mickey asked as his friend walked into the newspaper offices that evening.

"Excellent!" Goofy said happily. "The movie was really funny—and I ate six buckets of popcorn!"

"That's great," Mickey said. "But did you manage to find the man in the polka-dotted cap? Did you see what was inside the package that Peg Leg Pete delivered to him?"

"Well, uh . . ." Goofy hedged, "you know, it's always dark in a movie theater. Besides there were so many people, and the Panorama is so huge. . . ."

Mickey stared at his friend. "What?" he demanded. "You went to the Panorama? But I told you to go to the Oscar!"

"Oh . . . yeah." Goofy grinned sheepishly. "But I'd already seen all of the movies at the Oscar."

"Oh, no!" Mickey groaned. "Now our case against Peg Leg Pete is totally ruined."

Goofy looked at his shoes. "I'm sorry, Mickey," he said.

Mickey sighed. "That's all right." Mickey gave his friend a pat on the back. "Tomorrow morning I'll go find Inspector Craven. I have another idea that just might work."

The next morning, Mickey walked through the front doors of Police Headquarters. When Inspector Craven noticed the detective, he pretended to be carefully studying some papers on his desk.

"What do you want?" the inspector grumbled as Mickey stepped into his private office. "Can't you see that I'm busy? I've got work to do here!"

"Oh, I won't take up much of your time, Inspector," Mickey said cheerfully. "I just came to tell you that someone saw Peg Leg Pete giving one of your men a huge stack of money. I'm not sure, but it looks like a bribe to me. I've decided to tell all in the pages of my newspaper."

"No . . . you can't!" The inspector stood up so quickly that he sent the papers on his desk flying. "You have no idea whether there

was money in that envelope or not!"

Mickey smiled. "I never said the money was in an *envelope*," he pointed out. The detective turned toward the door. "The only way you could have known about the envelope is if it was delivered to you. Thanks for giving yourself away, Inspector. You've made my job much easier."

Back at the paper, Mickey closed himself into his office to work on the report for the investigation.

A little while later he heard a knock at the door. It was a man wearing rumpled clothes and an old-fashioned derby cap.

"Sorry to barge in on you," the man said. "My name is Max Pro, and I'm the sportswriter for the newspaper."

"Nice to meet you, Max," Mickey replied. "Have a seat. Editor Noble has told me you're one of the best reporters in the newsroom."

"That's very kind. The truth is," the sportswriter said, "I came to find you to . . . you know that story you've been working on?"

"Do you have some information for me?" Mickey asked.

"Well, like the rest of my colleagues, I really want to save *The Herald*. That's why I'd like to introduce you to someone I know, someone who has some very interesting information to share."

"And what is this person's name?" Mickey asked curiously.

"His name is Scoop, and he works for *The Tribune*, our main competitor. He has something to tell you. But it's better if he explains it to you in person. And one more thing before I go: when you want to win the game, you have to react at the right moment. Don't wait too long. Do you know what I mean?"

"You can count on me, Max, and thanks for the—"

But the sports reporter had already disappeared.

A half an hour later, Scoop walked into the newsroom.

After asking Scoop to make himself comfortable, Mickey sat down behind his desk. "I've decided to expose the whole story,"

Mickey announced. "And this time Peg Leg Pete is not going to get away with it!"

"I wish that were true." Scoop sighed. "He's got to be stopped—he's held the city in his grip for too long. But that crook won't be behind bars for long with just the evidence that you and your colleagues have collected. Believe me, there's a lot more."

"What do you know?" Mickey asked.

"Well, the newspaper I work for has gathered a lot of information on this group of criminals. But, unlike Mr. Noble, our editor in chief is afraid of them and doesn't want to publish what he knows. So we're sitting on a ton of evidence. For example, Peg Leg Pete's men ransacked a jewelry store that had refused their protection. And believe me, he's done much worse. The owner of La Colonna Restaurant told me about what happened when he refused the services of Lookout Security. They destroyed La Colonna's refrigerators so that all of the meat and produce rotted. The owner had to close the restaurant for ten days and he lost a lot of money."

"Scoop, this is dynamite!" Mickey declared.

His eyes twinkled with excitement. "Now we just have to gather some proof. Do you have any other leads?"

"Well . . . there's something strange going on with the company that the city's hired to clean the garbage off the streets. I've always asked myself how it was that the contract was given to Wash-All, Inc., because their employees are the most incompetent I've ever seen. I smell something fishy there, but I've never been able to find out where exactly the stench is coming from."

"Wherever you can smell something rotten, Peg Leg Pete's usually not far behind," Mickey agreed. "Now all I need is some evidence!"

Chapter 6

DIRTY DEALS AT CITY HALL

The following day, Mickey presented himself very early at the Brilliantine Cleaning Company, the company that held the cleaning contract with the city before it was given to dirty Wash-All, Inc. The owner, Richard Brilliant, was a white-haired man who wore a spotless white shirt, white pants, and white sneakers.

"What can I do for you?" he asked Detective Mickey, smiling to reveal a perfect set of pearly white teeth. "Are you interested in our Spring Cleaning package?"

"Not exactly. Let's just say that I'm working on a very particular kind of cleanup. I am trying to cleanse the city of corruption."

Mr. Brilliant looked insulted. "Well, you have the wrong address," he snapped. "I can assure you that at Brilliantine Cleaning Company you won't find corruption of any kind. My employees' records are spotless, and our accounting books are white as snow. Our business practices are utterly clean."

"Calm down," Mickey reassured him. "I believe you. I would just like to know how Wash-All was chosen to handle the city's cleaning contracts instead of Brilliantine. . . ."

Mr. Brilliant became white with rage.

"Why, yes . . . let's talk about it!" he fumed. "It's a disgrace! I offered my services, of course, and at a very reasonable price. I am sure that there was some sort of shady dealing involved. One of the city officials made sure that Wash-All got the contract, even though they are incompetent *and* scandalously expensive. Way over the going market rates. The city will be ruined—and filthy!"

Mr. Brilliant took a copy of the proposal

his company had made to City Hall from his desk. He showed the proposal to Mickey and added, "Look at this. Does it seem normal to you that such a reasonably priced proposal was refused? It seems pretty fishy to me, especially considering it came from us, the most trusted cleaning company in town."

"That's why I came to you," Mickey agreed. "I'm determined to expose this scandal. . . . But I need your help."

"You can count on it . . . I'll do whatever I can. What exactly do you need to know?"

"First I need to get the name of the city official who hired Wash-All for the contract."

"I am almost sure that his name was Mr. Hammer. He's an unpleasant man, very snobby. . . . He's a friend of this guy named Peg Leg Pete."

Mickey's jaw dropped. "Peg Leg Pete! Him again! I should've known. . . ."

Mr. Brilliant looked interested. "Do you know him?"

"Unfortunately, I do," Mickey admitted. "He's a real crook! Mr. Brilliant, would you be able to give me a copy of the proposal you presented to City Hall, as well as their letter of refusal. . . . I'll print both in *The Herald*. People have a right to know what their city government is doing."

Mr. Brilliant went straight to his files and found the documents Mickey was looking for. "Here they are," he said to the detective. "Please take good care of them."

"I will," Mickey promised. "They'll go into tomorrow's early edition."

The next day the newsstands were over-run. *The Herald* kept selling out, and Donald Duck spent the morning running back and forth from the newspaper offices to replenish the supply. By 11 A.M., there were no more papers in *The Herald* offices—the edition had sold out.

The streets were abuzz with talk about Wash-All, Inc. People were furious that their tax money had been used to pay off a company of cheats.

But who was the director of this company? Everyone wanted to know why he hadn't come forward to defend himself.

Mickey was determined to find out. The moment the paper had gone to press, he looked up the address and headed straight for the offices of Wash-All, Inc.

The company was located on a dark and narrow street. The building looked like it was about to fall apart—the windows were filthy with fingerprints, and the carpet inside looked like it hadn't been vacuumed in years.

This is supposed to be a *cleaning* company? Mickey thought as he stood in the lobby.

The man at the reception desk wore wrinkled, dirty clothes, and his fingernails were black with grime. He was eating a cheese sandwich . . . noisily.

"Good morning," Detective Mickey said. "I'd like to speak with your manager."

"He's not here," the man said as crumbs from his sandwich fell over his desk. "He's never here. I take care of everything."

"I see. . . ." Mickey said. He doubted that this man took care of anything, but he chose not to say so. "Well, would you give me the name of your boss? I'll just give him a call."

The man cocked an eyebrow. "Sorry, mister, but I have strict orders—the boss doesn't want to speak with anyone—"

The telephone rang, cutting him off. "*Excuse* me," the man said as he picked up the phone. Mickey understood from the man's voice that he wanted Mickey to leave. Mickey turned and walked out the front door. But the detective thought that there might be a few clues in the Wash-All offices. Once he was out in the street, Mickey slipped back in through a window that someone had left open.

In the next room, the man at the desk was talking on the phone. Mickey barely recognized his voice, which had suddenly become *very* polite.

"Certainly, Mr. Hammer," the man said. "I'll get it to you immediately. Mr. Peg Leg Pete instructed me that you were not to be kept waiting. . . . When can you meet him? Very good, sir! . . . I'll call him this minute. . . . I'll let him know. Very well, Mr. Councilman . . . Good-bye."

The man hung up the phone and punched in a number. He waited a moment, then said, "Boss, Hammer just called. He wants to see you as soon as possible. He says it's urgent."

Mickey smiled. It looked like Scoop was right—Peg Leg Pete *was* in on this whole filthy business. And Councilman Hammer was his accomplice.

It didn't matter . . . city official or not, Mickey would see that they were all put away for good. And then, when they were all in prison, Hammer, Peg Leg Pete, and that spineless Inspector Craven could all play cards together. . . .

Chapter 7

THE BOSS'S PIZZA

Back at the newsroom, Mickey picked up the phone and punched in a number.

"Congratulations!" the detective said when Peg Leg Pete answered. "I heard that the mayor signed a great contract with your company. Have you decided it's finally time to start making an honest living?"

"My company?" Peg Leg Pete asked innocently. "I don't know what you're talking about."

"Drop the act, Pete," Mickey growled. "I've got evidence tying you to Wash-All, Inc."

"Oh, *that* company," Peg Leg Pete said smoothly. "That's right. I'm going to help clean up this city. The streets will shine when my employees are finished with them."

"You and I both know that the only way the streets will shine is if they learn to clean themselves. Because your company won't do anything—"

The phone clicked as Peg Leg Pete hung up on Mickey. The detective shrugged. It was pointless to try to get Peg Leg Pete to come clean, anyway.

"Peg Leg Pete needs to be sent to prison, where they'll put a mop in his hands and show him what cleaning up is all about. . . ." Mickey muttered.

"Don't get upset," Minnie said to her grumbling partner. "You should take me to the movies instead. That way we can distract ourselves for a little while. At the Oscar Cinema they're showing a film that's—"

"Sorry, Minnie," Mickey said, interrupting her as he typed a few notes into his newly fixed computer, "I'm not in the right mood to go to the movies. I can't concentrate on

anything else until this case is solved. If only
I could get into Peg Leg Pete's house. . . ."

"Get into his house? Why would you want
to do that?" Minnie asked.

"To get my hands on that fantastic contract
that the city offered him. He's the head of
Wash-All, Inc., so he must keep copies of all
their important papers. I need proof of his
dishonesty . . . and Hammer's."

"But you'll never get into his house," Minnie pointed out.

Mickey smiled. "I'll find a way, you'll see!" he said confidently. "In the meantime, I have to study his movements. I need to know when he usually goes out of his apartment."

Minnie folded her arms across her chest. "How will you find time to do that *and* research the case *and* publish the newspaper?"

"Good point," Mickey admitted. "I know! I'll ask Goofy to keep an eye on him."

"Well, then, now that you've solved that problem, do you think we can go see that movie at the Oscar Cinema?" Minnie asked.

"The Oscar . . ." Mickey said, a look of alarm crossing his face. "I'd forgotten about that."

Minnie knew what Mickey was thinking. He was remembering how he had asked Goofy to go on that stakeout at the Oscar Cinema. And Goofy had goofed—big time!

"Well," Mickey said, shaking his head, "I really don't have a choice. You and I have too much work to do here. Goofy is the only one who's free to follow Pete. I'll just make sure to give him very clear instructions this time."

Three days later, Goofy was giving Mickey his report on Peg Leg Pete's movements. "He comes . . . and he goes. . . ." Goofy said.

"Um, Goofy . . ." Mickey hesitated. He didn't want to hurt his friend's feelings. "Do you think you could be a bit more precise? Did you notice his schedule at all?"

"Of course," Goofy said proudly. "I wrote down everything he did in this notebook."

"Great!" Mickey grinned. "Okay, give me an example. Tell me what he did yesterday morning."

"Okeydokey. I'll turn to the page for yesterday. . . . All right—he opened the window at ten-fifteen. He went out to get a newspaper at ten-fifteen. He came back at ten-fifteen. . . . Hey!" Goofy said. "He does everything at the same time!"

"Er—" Mickey said. "I think you'd better check your watch."

Goofy held up his wrist. "Gawrsh!" he said. "It's ten-fifteen right now. What a coincidence!"

"I think maybe your watch is *broken*," Mickey suggested.

"Aw, shucks," Goofy said as he noticed that the second hand wasn't moving. "You're right."

"Okay, let's do this," Detective Mickey said with a sigh. "You go get your watch fixed. Then go back to Peg Leg Pete's house tomorrow morning and write down all of his movements. I'll take over at lunchtime."

The next day, Mickey met up with Goofy across the street from Peg Leg Pete's house. They had just crouched between two parked cars when a man passed by walking very quickly. He was carrying a pizza box in his hands—and was headed for Peg Leg Pete's door.

"Hey!" Mickey whispered. "Who's that?"

"It's a pizza delivery boy," Goofy replied.

Mickey rolled his eyes. "I just wanted to know if you've seen him here before."

"Oh!" Goofy said. "Sure! He comes here every day around lunchtime."

"Very interesting!" Mickey declared. "This

is perfect. Now I know how we can get into Peg Leg Pete's house. Goofy, have you noticed what restaurant he's from, by any chance?"

"Oh, sure! They make the best pizza in the city. Wacky Pizza."

"Hmm," Mickey said. "We've got to find out what kind of pizza he orders. . . ."

"Easy!" Goofy exclaimed, and searched his pockets for his cell phone. He punched in a number. "Hello? Wacky Pizza?" Goofy said. "Hi, it's Peg Leg Pete. I wanted to make sure you had my pizza order for tomorrow. And is it the kind I like? Well, what kind is that? Pepperoni? Of course! No, no, I don't want to change my order; I was just testing you. But you got it right—good job! Thanks!"

Goofy grinned. "Peg Leg Pete orders pepperoni pizza every day."

"Great job, Goofy!" Mickey said, giving his friend a pat on the back. "Then *we'll* get a pepperoni pizza, too."

"Well, I don't know," Goofy said. "Pepperoni can be kind of greasy. . . ."

Mickey chuckled. "Don't worry, it's not for us! Just go and buy a pepperoni pizza from

Wacky Pizza tomorrow morning at eleven-thirty, and bring it to me at the newspaper. Got it? Come on, let's get back to the newsroom. We're running late."

Chapter 8

SWEET DREAMS, PEG LEG PETE!

A few minutes before noon the next day, Mickey walked up the street in front of Peg Leg Pete's house. He had to be careful to turn the corner at just the right moment.

Mickey heard the delivery boy's rubber-soled shoes squeaking as he approached. Mickey quickened his pace. . . and ran head-first into the pizza boy as they both arrived at the corner.

"Oh, I'm sorry!" Mickey cried as the pizza boy fell and the pizza went flying. Or rather,

the pizzas. Mickey, of course, had been carrying an identical box containing a nearly identical pizza.

"Why don't you watch where you're going?" the delivery boy demanded. He picked himself up and looked at the pizzas, which were lying on the grass. "Look at that! Now my customer is going to yell at me—he has such a bad temper!"

"I'm really very sorry," Mickey said. "But look—the box didn't even come open. It'll be all right ... your customer never has to know." Mickey picked up the box that he'd been carrying and handed it to the pizza boy. Then Mickey took the one that the pizza boy had been delivering, and smiled to himself. Peg Leg Pete would soon be devouring Mickey's pizza. That was too bad for him, because Mickey had made sure that there were mushrooms in the pizza sauce. And Mickey knew from a previous case he'd worked on against Peg Leg Pete that the criminal was highly allergic to mushrooms. They didn't make him sick, they just made him very, very sleepy. . . .

Once Peg Leg Pete was snoring away, Mickey and Goofy slipped quietly into Peg Leg Pete's house. The scoundrel was sprawled out along the length of his desk asleep, his nose still stuck in the pizza. The mushrooms had made him so sleepy that he hadn't even finished it.

"It's a pity to see such a good pizza go to waste," Goofy commented. "Could we just have a piece or two?"

"We didn't come here for lunch—it's time to get to work. We have to find those documents before this crook wakes up."

Keeping their ears open to make sure Peg Leg Pete was still snoring, Mickey and Goofy turned the apartment upside down. Finally, they found what they were looking for—the contract between Peg Leg Pete and the city, together with a letter from Mr. Hammer.

A very interesting letter . . .

Chapter 9

PEG LEG PETE BLOWS UP

"Aaaah . . . I'm sooo . . . sleepy!" Peg Leg Pete sighed and stretched.

He opened his eyes and looked at the clock. "What time is it?" he asked groggily. "Six o'clock? How could I have fallen asleep without even finishing my favorite pizza?"

He noticed that something strange had happened in the house while he was asleep. All of his desk drawers were open. And the pile of mail that had been on the armchair was scattered all over the room . . . how weird!

Peg Leg Pete got up slowly from his chair

and walked into the bedroom. Everything was upside down. Even the files full of documents that had been piled neatly under the bed were in complete disarray.

"Aha!" Peg Leg Pete shouted. "Someone searched my house! And that someone can't be anyone other than that nosy Mickey Mouse! He'd better not have gotten his hands on that contract with the city or on Hammer's letter—that would be a disaster!"

The crook rushed to the bathroom and grabbed the dirty-clothes hamper. Dirty pants, socks, and shirts went flying. . . .

Finally he found the envelope he was looking for. It was still fat. Great! Peg Leg Pete thought. That means the documents are safe inside.

Peg Leg Pete let out a laugh.

"Dear Councilman Hammer!" he said. "Wait until you see how I clean up this city! And if I could just clean up Mickey Mouse and his annoying little friends, the place would *really* be spotless. . . ."

Sneering, the criminal opened the envelope. He wanted to look at the numbers on

the contract again, so he could think about how rich he was about to be....

"Wait a minute! What's going on—the documents aren't here! That pest Mickey replaced them with ... a copy of *The Herald*!" Peg Leg Pete groaned. Now Detective Mickey would reveal every sordid detail of his deal with the city in the next day's paper. Everyone would know the truth!

"Well, now I have no choice," Peg Leg Pete concluded. "It's time to shut that newspaper down for good! But how?" Peg Leg Pete scratched his chin, deep in thought. "I know!" he said suddenly. "I'll burn down the newsroom, and all of the documents with it. Without those documents, they can't prove a thing!"

Meanwhile, the newsroom at *The Herald* was a hive of activity.

The next day's edition had to be perfect—it was the finale that would finally uncover the entire filthy scandal, and with documented proof. Mickey had organized a special meeting. They needed to plan the front-page article, choose the photographs, decide on a headline. . . .

"I have an idea for a headline," Goofy said. " 'The Hammer-Peg Scandal.' "

"It's a little confusing," Minnie replied gently.

After a hot debate, the news staff decided to dedicate a special extra edition to the dirty scandal with the full-page headline: "Shocking Revelations."

Much later that night, Mickey and Minnie were finally preparing to go home. They had just closed the computer file that contained the special edition and were preparing to send it to the printer.

The newsroom had the latest technology. During the night, all their work would be transmitted electronically to the printer. Early the next morning, even before the journalists arrived in the newsroom, the paper would be waiting for them, hot off the presses.

Minnie was more than ready to go. She had already been waiting quite a while in front of Mickey's office door and was beginning to tap her foot impatiently.

"What are you doing in there, Mickey?" she asked with a yawn. "Aren't we finished with tomorrow's paper?"

"I'm coming," Mickey replied. He closed a file cabinet drawer and reached for his coat. "So, do you want to go see a movie now?" he asked as they left the building. "It's been a long time since we've had a moment to relax."

The two detectives had just turned the

corner on their way to the cinema when they heard a huge explosion. The sky was suddenly filled with flames. They heard someone shout: "What happened? Where was the explosion?"

Mickey and Minnie ran toward the scene, which was in the direction they'd come from. As they turned a corner, Minnie gasped. The newsroom was on fire. A squadron of firefighters was already hard at work.

"On no!" Minnie sighed. "A fuse box must've blown. . . ."

"Fuse box?" Mickey asked doubtfully. "I don't think so."

"You're right," she conceded. "Of course . . . this is the work of Peg Leg Pete."

The firefighters weren't allowing anyone to come close to the building. It didn't really matter, though. Mickey and Minnie already knew that all their work had been lost.

"What a catastrophe!" Minnie exclaimed dejectedly. "The printer won't have received even half of what we transmitted. The special edition won't be able to come out! It's so unfair! The crooks always get the last word. . . ."

"Do you really think so?" Mickey replied, as he pulled a thick mailing envelope from his bag. "Do you remember that I made you wait for me in the newsroom while I finished up some things?"

Minnie nodded.

"I copied all of our work onto disks," Mickey explained. "You can never be too careful. Especially when you're dealing with a scoundrel like Peg Leg Pete. Now all we have to do is run these over to the printer by hand. You'll see, the special edition will be on the newsstands tomorrow morning."

"Oh, Mickey!" Minnie gave the detective a kiss on the cheek, making him blush. "Let's hurry up and print the edition of the century!"

Chapter 10

A FINAL CLEANUP

The next day, the sales of *The Herald* were off the charts.

"Did you read *The Herald*?" people asked each other on the street. "It's an amazing edition! Like a detective novel!"

"It looks like Hammer's been caught red-handed. They published a letter with his signature thanking Peg Leg Pete for his 'generous campaign contribution.'"

"Who would've thought? Councilman Hammer is such a high-profile figure! You can't trust anyone these days."

"It's a good thing they got Mickey Mouse on the case! He and Minnie are really excellent detectives!"

Of all the readers of the special edition, none was more shocked than the mayor. The moment he finished reading, he searched his office for the file called "Cleanup" and opened it. But it was empty! Hammer had disposed of the evidence. What a fool. How could he think that he wouldn't eventually get caught?

The mayor decided to pay a visit to Mickey Mouse.

"Congratulations on your fine work!" he said, as he pumped Mickey's hand up and down vigorously. "And you completed your investigation in record time."

"You are too kind, Mr. Mayor," Mickey replied humbly.

"And to think that I had complete trust in that Hammer!" The mayor shook his head. "Naturally I'll have him arrested as soon as possible. I'm going to call Inspector Craven immediately and have him taken away."

"For goodness' sakes, no! I'd would like to

ask that you wait until you read the paper tomorrow, when you'll get the real lowdown on Inspector Craven....The Hammer scandal has kept me so busy that I haven't had time to think about Craven, but I'll wrap up my investigation today."

The mayor looked shocked. "He's involved in this whole scandal, too?"

"I'm afraid so," Mickey replied. "Among

other things, he took a bribe from Peg Leg Pete in exchange for letting him out of jail."

"Thank you for telling me. . . I'll have all of these 'upstanding citizens' arrested immediately. Inspector Sharp should never have retired. I know him: he was a man who loved his work. Who knows? Maybe I could convince him to come back."

Arrest warrants for the crooks were issued right away, and Inspector Craven and Councilman Hammer were immediately suspended from duty.

But Mickey was still on edge. The mayor let Detective Mickey know every time someone was arrested, but days passed and the dirtiest criminal of all still hadn't been caught—Peg Leg Pete!

A few days later, the mayor showed up for a visit with Mickey and gave him the news he'd been waiting for.

"Unfortunately, Sharp didn't feel up to coming back to work," he said regretfully. "But now a young, courageous, and, above all, honest youngster has taken his place. He took the investigation into his own hands and it wasn't long before we saw results. Wash-All, Inc. is closed down forever. And of course Lookout Security Services will suffer the same fate. Everyone in the city seems to be breathing easier now that Peg Leg Pete is under lock and key!"

"That's great!" Mickey exclaimed. "But I know that crook well. Sooner or later he'll try to escape . . . and we have to be ready for him. I'll be waiting, I can promise you that!"

EPILOGUE

"A drink to Mickey!" Minnie exclaimed holding up her cup of lemonade. "I'm so proud of him!"

"To Mickey!" everyone shouted.

Mickey had ordered food from Wacky Pizza for everyone.

"This is really great pizza!" Goofy raved. "May Mickey's paper have a long run!" He took another huge bite out of his slice.

"What do you mean, 'Mickey's paper'?" the investigator asked. "Of course, I've enjoyed my little stint as a journalist, but that was just part of my work as a detective. And now that our city is clean again, so to speak, I

daresay that my journalistic career has come to an end. I know that Mr. Noble has called back the reporters who had left because of Peg Leg Pete's threats . . . now it's time for Minnie and me to return to the Mickey and Minnie Detective Agency."

"Too bad," Goofy said. "Our little adventure could have made us famous."

"What if it already has?" Mickey grinned.

"What are you talking about?" Clarabelle asked curiously.

"Look at this. Hot off the press." Mickey pulled the next day's edition of the paper out of his pocket. He unfolded it, and held it up. On the front page, there was a full-page profile of the Mickey and Minnie Detective Agency's team of intrepid reporters.

Everyone gathered around to get a closer look.

"Not bad!" Horace commented.

"Not bad? You mean *great*!" Minnie corrected him. "Let's have another toast—to our wonderful team!"

FROM Mickey Mysteries

ABRACADABRA

Chapter 1

COMPANY'S COMING

Goofy arrived at the office with a big white bakery box.

"Wow! This looks delicious!" Minnie said as they opened the box. Pink and white sugar-roses sat on top of thick layers of creamy chocolate frosting.

"I can't wait to have a slice!" said Goofy, licking his lips.

Mickey smiled. He didn't know anyone

who had a bigger sweet tooth than Goofy.

When they were done, Minnie stood up. "Well, now that it's lunchtime, I'm going home for a bit," she announced. "But I'm sure you won't want to eat lunch after that! Too bad, because I made you two some of my famous—"

"Wait a minute!" Mickey cut her off. "Don't think we're going to pass up lunch! We'll just eat it a little later than usual, that's all." Mickey grinned, then added, "You go on ahead, Minnie. Since Goofy is here, I'm going to have him help me put some documents in order in the top storage files. That is, if he can manage to get up out of his chair after all the cake he's eaten. We'll meet you at your place in half an hour or so."

"Great!" Minnie said, picking up her purse. "See you real soon!" she sang as she walked out the door.

"So," Goofy said once Minnie had left, "where are those files you needed help with?"

"To tell the truth," Mickey began, "I don't really need help with the files. I was hoping you would come with me somewhere."

"Where?" asked Goofy.

"Well," said Mickey mysteriously, "Minnie's birthday is two weeks from Saturday. I've been trying to think of a gift for her, something really special, but I couldn't come up with anything. Then I found out about a new amusement park called Enigma. It's a mystery theme park. I'm sure she'll love it! Will you come with me to the travel agency so I can get tickets?"

"Sure," said Goofy.

Mickey dug around in his desk and pulled out a pamphlet. "Take a look at this brochure—they have a wax museum, a haunted house, a ride on a ghost train, detective movies, and overnight accommodations in this gloomy castle. It sounds really spooky and fun! I'm going to get two tickets for the package deal. . . ."

Mickey got so excited about the mystery theme park that he lost track of time. Before he knew it, it was already 1:30.

"Oh, no!" Mickey said, catching sight of the clock. "I didn't realize it was so late. Now there's no time to get the tickets before we meet Minnie for lunch. Oh, well. I guess we can just pass by the travel agency later in the afternoon."

"Okeydokey," Goofy replied. "Now let's go meet Minnie."

It was a short walk to the street where Minnie lived, and Mickey and Goofy arrived there in no time. But as they turned the corner, someone walked briskly past Goofy, shoving him. Goofy fell facedown on the pavement!

A large man with long, jet-black hair and a mustache, his face half covered by an enormous pair of black sunglasses, kept striding down the sidewalk. He didn't look back— and he didn't even say he was sorry!

"That was so rude!" Mickey fumed. He held out his hand and helped his friend to his feet.

"Tell me about it," Goofy agreed as he brushed himself off.

Goofy took a moment to straighten himself out, then the two friends headed up Minnie's front walk. Mickey rang the doorbell. No answer. Mickey and Goofy looked at

one another, worried. Without saying a word, they went around back to see if she was in the yard and hadn't heard the doorbell.

Suddenly, Detective Mickey broke into a run.

"Minnie!" he shouted. "Minnie! What's wrong?"

Minnie was lying on the ground. She was

pale, and she seemed to be unconscious. Mickey felt her pulse and put his hand to her forehead.

"She doesn't have a fever. And her heart rate seems normal." Mickey turned to his friend. "Goofy, run and get a glass of water."

Goofy nodded and rushed into Minnie's house through the back door. When he returned, Mickey took the glass of water and immediately splashed it on Minnie's face.

Minnie's eyes popped open. "That's a nice way to thank someone who's invited you over for lunch!" she said, glaring at Mickey.

"But Minnie, you fainted and—"

"Fainted?" Minnie demanded. "I've never fainted in my life. I can't believe you think you can fool me with your jokes twice in one day."

"Minnie, believe me," Goofy interrupted, "you were flat on your back in the grass—"

"That's enough!" Minnie cried, exasperated. "I know better than to believe you two jokers. Well, too bad for you—I officially take back my lunch invitation!"